For Mum and Dad—my first and forever home. C.A.

First edition for the United States and Canada published in 2018
by Barron's Educational Series, Inc.

First published in Great Britain in 2018 by Anderson Press Ltd.
Text copyright © Corrinne Averiss, 2018.
Illustration copyright © Susan Varley, 2018.

All inquiries should be addressed to:
Barron's Educational Series, Inc.
250 Wireless Boulevard
Hauppauge, NY 11788
www.barronseduc.com

ISBN: 978-1-4380-5056-0

Library of Congress Control No.: 2017960547

Date of Manufacture: May 2018
Manufactured by: Tien Wah Press, Johor, Malaysia

Printed in Malaysia
9 8 7 6 5 4 3 2 1

SORREL
and the
SLEEPOVER

Corrinne Averiss

Susan Varley

BARRON'S

Sorrel had never had a friend who was just the same,
until she met Sage. They liked the same games, sang the
same songs, and said the same things at the same time.
They even had the same…

...stripe on their tails!

It was the luckiest, most perfect thing,
to share with a friend who's just the same.
So Sage invited Sorrel to a sleepover at her house.

It was Sorrel's first night away from home.
Mom helped her pack her little nutshell
with all the things she might need.

"Are you nervous?" asked Mom.
"Oh no," said Sorrel, "because Sage
and I are just the same!"

Sage's home was woody
and wide, solid and strong.
There were aunties in the east
nest and cousins in the west.

Branches that went on forever, peppered
with pine cones and the softest green needles.
Sorrel was amazed—Sage was so lucky!

Sorrel and Sage snuggled up as the sun went down.
"I can't wait to stay at your house next time,"
said Sage as they fell asleep.

But while Sage snoozed, Sorrel squirmed…
her home was not like this at all.

Sorrel's home was small and slim,
its branches were broken and bumpy,
and it wobbled in the wind.

There were no uncles, no grandmas, no brothers
or sisters…just Sorrel and her mom.

She decided not to invite Sage to a sleepover at her house.
Best friends don't have differences, thought Sorrel.
She wanted Sage to think they were just the same.

But Sage didn't forget about the sleepover easily—she even packed her nutshell. Sorrel had to make up excuses: "We can't have a sleepover at my house, because…"

"Because my mom's very sick. She ate a bad nut.
It made her face go green and her nose go red.
She needs peace and quiet while she stays in bed!"

"Because two dozen cousins are coming to stay.
Their bags, shoes, and coats take up so much space,
there's no room to have friends at our place."

"Because our root-pipe burst yesterday.
The plumber said it will take days to repair.
You can't stay over, there's water everywhere!"

"We can't have a sleepover at my tree because…"

"Because?" sighed Sage.

"Because…we've painted it pink! It took us all day.

So the leaves are too wet for an overnight stay."

"PINK?" said Sage.

"Er…yes," replied Sorrel.

One day, Sage and Sorrel were playing hide-n-squeak when
a breeze brought a flutter of pink petals their way.

"Pink—let's follow them!" said Sage, scampering toward a
pink tree. "This must be your home. It's so…BEAUTIFUL."

Sorrel was shocked. Sage didn't notice that the branches
were broken and bumpy or that it wobbled in the wind.
Her mom invited Sage to stay for tea.

"Your pink paint is perfect," said Sage.

"Paint?" said Sorrel's mom. "Our cherry tree always grows pink blossoms."

Sorrel had some explaining to do. "I'm sorry I lied," she said.

"I thought if you came to my tree and saw it was so different

from yours, you wouldn't be my friend."

"It doesn't matter that it's not the same," laughed Sage.

"You're so lucky to be different, Sorrel! I don't know

anyone else who sleeps in pink clouds."

That night, Sorrel and Sage enjoyed their best
sleepover yet in a cherry blossom bed. Sharing the
same blanket, watching the same petals,
they were the friendliest of friends.

As Sage snoozed, Sorrel smiled.
It was the luckiest, most perfect thing,
to share something different with
a friend who's just the same.